# ZOMBIE ZERO
## THE SHORT STORIES

## THE
## BEGINNING OF THE END

Zombie Zero: The Short Stories
The Beginning of the End



ISBN-13: 978-1-944916-96-1
ISBN-10: 1-944916-96-2

**www.SuddenInsightPublishing.com**
Indie publishing for the Indie Author

# ZOMBIE ZERO
## THE SHORT STORIES

# THE
# BEGINNING OF THE END

# J.K. NORRY

# FOREWORD

The 'Year of the Zombie' continues with 'The Beginning of the End'. If you don't care about the order these come in, neither do I; the short stories can be read in any sequence you like. If you want to read these in the order they are intended to be read in, there are two books you should have read at this point.

The first is 'Zombie Zero: The First Zombie'. It is the main story in all of this, offering up the deeper meaning of this popular monster. Like a tall tree sprouting, this story had many branches. Rather than publish one huge meandering volume, we decided to make eight smaller ones. Six of those are the short story books, one of which you are reading right now. The other two are that main trunk I mentioned, which will reach its full towering height in 'Zombie Zero: The Last Zombie'.

The other book you will want to have read at this point is 'The Sickness Spreads'. It's the first volume in the 'Zombie Zero' short stories.

The main reason for this sequencing is because it fleshes out the story in the first book best this way. Things go a whole new weird direction in the last book, but we'll talk about that when the time is right. Now, let's talk about these short stories, and assume you're all caught up.

But first, my usual disclaimer: the introductory matter and messages between the stories are not something you need to read, if you don't want to. When my favorite authors write long forewords, afterwords and between-story commentary, I love it. Some folks don't, and I understand. If you are here for zombie stories, I'm happy to say we got the goods! Look for the three pages that say 'Prologue Prequel', 'John's Stones' and 'Tina's Bedside', and read from there. You won't offend me by not being interested in anything but the stories, if I won't offend you indulging readers like me.

With that out of the way, let's talk a little more about how this whole thing came together. It wasn't long ago that I expected to be writing fantasy for some time to come. When 2015 was wrapping up, I took a good long look at all the stories vying for my time and attention. What cried out the loudest, to my surprise, were the zombies.

# ABOUT THE SHORT STORIES

First things first: there are no spoilers here, nor will there be in any of the in-between matter. I'll assume you've read the previous story in this book, but nothing else. I hate spoilers, and I wouldn't do that to you.

I will tell you what chapter these stories tie into in the book, but only by number. I'll also tell you that the characters in these short stories do play feature roles in 'Zombie Zero: The First Zombie'; I share that because it is my reason for releasing this set as the second volume. If you've read the book, these will provide some more back and between stories. If you haven't read the book, no worries; these stories stand alone, even when they weave together.

When a whole world is falling apart, there are a lot of things going on. My primary focus was on the main story, at first; then these others began to speak to me, and I knew I had to write them. All eighteen of them. At first, I thought it would be fun to just share them with newsletter subscribers as bonus content. Cool idea, right?

Then the stories started taking shape, and I knew they couldn't just live at my secret society's secret online headquarters. I needed to share these with the world, and let folks who liked the book have access to them. It was kind of rude to assume that everyone knew about the secret society, or wanted an e-mail from a weirdo like me every week. Also, these weren't just filler content; they were great stories. The more they complemented the book, the more I knew they had to see print.

The first thing that came to mind when I realized these would be best as six smaller books were my childhood summers. I remembered the sci-fi and horror magazines that I used to devour as a young teen; they were often small enough to fit in your pocket, the stories printed on thin paper and the covers graced with unusually compelling art. They had the wildest stories in them, often by different authors; and the cover art, though fantastic, never seemed to have anything to do with any of the actual stories.

I loved the thought immediately: I could use the same basic formula, only make it my own. Good thing we had picked the right artist. I'd like to tell you a little about him, and how much he made this all come to life.

# ODE TO SEAN HARRINGTON

I hope you had a good long look at that cover, whether you got the print or ebook version. Take a minute now, if you want; it's totally worth another look, and I'll be here when you get back.

That art is by Sean Harrington. I gave him descriptions of the stories, and told him I was thinking of the kind of art that had been on the pulp publications I had loved so much as a kid. That was it, and he was off. Sean delivered these pieces to us every couple of weeks, and we whooped and hollered enthusiastically every time we saw a new one come in. Each concept comes from his mind, and the art comes from his hands; and I can honestly say I couldn't have thought of better covers for these books. The art goes perfectly with the overall theme, as well as with the individual stories.

That was one of the things I didn't like about those old pulp magazines: I always wished the art was a little more relatable to at least one of the stories.

The other thing that bugged me about those cool old publications was the cheap paper; I didn't want them to seem disposable, or easily recycled. I wanted them to be collectible. So the art is related to the stories here, and the paper is high quality on the print version. Otherwise, these short story collections are just what I wanted them to be: books with fantastic art that fit easily in a bag or back pocket.

The fantastic art part of that equation is all Sean, and I would be remiss not to mention that it was his style that helped give me the overall idea in the first place. Some of the art on those old publications was shocking in the most delightful way, unique stark imagery like I had never seen.

Thanks to Sean Harrington, all of the art in this series is the best of that style of magic. Also, they're related to the stories; you know, like they ought to be.

Sean is a pretty cool calm presence by e-mail; it's a nice counterpoint to the effusive and wordy messages I tend to send him. He probably thinks that his art totally speaks for itself, and properly represents what he has to say; I completely agree. My thanks go out to him, once again, for bringing the world of 'Zombie Zero' to life in a whole new way.

# ODE TO DAWN MARSHALL

Sometimes I say 'I' when talking about these projects, and other times I say 'we'. I am not referring to myself in the plural first person, in case you were starting to worry; I have a partner.

Her name is Dawn Marshall, and she is a huge part of why this book exists in the first place. She's also a huge part of why I'm such a happy guy, since I'm lucky enough to have her as my partner in all things.

It was Dawn who saw the path to publishing that we finally decided on, and put the business itself together. She learned all the technical aspects of making my books into something real, and now...well, here we are! With actual paved road behind us! Well, ahead of us anyway...

Most of what Dawn does goes without notice. It's a testament to how professionally she edits, formats and designs everything when no one pays special attention to what she does; the only time anyone mentions those fundamental aspects of a publication is when they're missing, or improperly done.

Dawn makes sure everything is smooth and clean and professional, so my books can be the best version of themselves they can be. All I have to do is write, my favorite thing to do!

Dawn also puts together bookmark and banner designs, all the ad copy for my books, and ways to produce all the fun things I so love to ask for. Buttons, book bags, custom pens, calling cards like no other...no matter how crazy my ideas, she finds ways to bring them out of my head and into the world.

Some ideas I can't have until she tells me what's possible; as soon as I want it, I want it now. No matter how many times I ask if something has arrived yet the day after she orders it, she always answers in the most calm manner.

Aside from being a bit of a saint, Dawn is also my muse. She never tires of hearing about the books I want to write someday, or the details about characters that only I know; I read blogs to her before I send them to her to post, and judge whether it's good or not based on her reaction. She doesn't always approve, and that's part of why I need her; sometimes it takes someone we love to help us say what we need to say. I am grateful that Dawn is that someone for me.

# ABOUT PROLOGUE PREQUEL

I'm going to talk about the first book here, to tell you what chapter this ties into and give you a little back story on this back story. It doesn't really count as a spoiler, for a couple reasons: first, you can read the prologue to 'Zombie Zero: The First Zombie' for free on my website, and that's all I'm talking about here. Second, it's not really much advance information; it's just me feeling free to talk about the publicly posted part of the book in here. Also, it's really quite relevant.

There are eighteen short stories altogether in this collection, to be released in six volumes. Some of the stories snuck up on me, or revealed themselves through other stories. That was not the case with this story. When I was writing the prologue to 'Zombie Zero: The First Zombie', I remember thinking how cool it would be to go back before even that incident happened, way back to when General Roberts was a sergeant who still believed there was no such thing as zombies. I really wanted to meet that guy.

Putting the thought aside, I got to work on the subsequent chapters. It happened again, of course, then a few more times; and by the time I was done writing I knew there had to be short stories to go with the long ones. Lots of them.

I created the files, in sets, and this was one of the first sets that were created and outlined. I saved it for last, though; this set was important in so many ways, I wanted to have plenty of time to think on the stories and let them speak to me.

All eighteen of them.

The other two stories in this set were started before this one. They're the other two in this book, of course. This being the last set, I had completed fifteen other short stories at this point. Once I got to writing in this one, I couldn't stop. I pushed right on through to the end, and decided immediately that I needed to share it with my newsletter subscribers the day the book released.

It created a cool slingshot effect, drawing back even further into the past to launch us right into the zombie apocalypse as it goes down in the book. It's also a pretty cool story on its own.

I hope you enjoy 'Prologue Prequel'.

And that you didn't just have lunch.

# PROLOGUE PREQUEL
## (THE GENERAL'S FIRST TIME)

The general cut the thin slab of delicious into small pieces, refusing to let his stomach turn. Tina would tolerate him coming home late; she would not stand for it if he came home hungry. Even more importantly, the meatloaf could not go uneaten. She would know that something was truly wrong then; that wouldn't be fair. There would be no throwing it away either, of course. For starters, it was Tina's meatloaf; nothing could ruin his taste for that. Second, she would know.

His wife had asked him to keep certain secrets from her years ago, for her sake; he had honored her wishes, and would continue to keep both his promise and those secrets. Everything else about him was an open book to her; Tina knew his thoughts better than he did, and there would be no lying to her about meatloaf. Or any other mundane matter.

Of course, he was not going to tell her about the zombies, or the murder.

Murders. Whatever.

The general pierced one of the small pieces with the tines of his fork, the one she had wrapped in a paper napkin and put in his cooler alongside the sliced piece of perfection. He held it up to his nose, let the cool scent drift into his nostrils.

His stomach rumbled, and not with churning disgust. The general sniffed again, and let a slow smile spread across his face while letting his thoughts drift to the distant past. It touched his tongue, the flavor exploding in his mouth while memories coalesced in his mind. The scene was as clear and sharp as the taste was soothing and invigorating. The general took another small bite before the first was finished, and let his thoughts go where they wanted to. It was still zombies; but the memory was twenty years old, and had settled into a palatable compartment for him.

Reflecting on it, the general realized that most folks shouldn't eat while recounting a story of this nature, or hearing someone recount it for them; he then thought that it was probably good that no one would ever hear the story. Only he had survived, after all; and the general would never tell, any more than he had been required to report.

Stabbing another tiny square of love in meat form, the general let his mind drift back completely.

* * *

"Sergeant, what the hell is this?" General Watts towered over his own desk, poked him in the chest.

The sergeant sighed.

"It's a recommendation, sir." The sergeant didn't back up; instead he let the older and smaller man poke his chest again. "If we implement this schedule, the security team will be far more effective in doing their jobs. I've also submitted a patrol plan; it covers more area with less troops, and will allow all restricted areas to have constant eyes on them. The schedule and the patrol plan together will allow us to provide more effective round the clock security with less hours logged."

General Watts looked down at the papers on his desk, shifted them.

"What do we do with all these extra hours?" Watts sniffed.

"They're not extra, sir," he responded. "The original schedule does not allow for time off. Everyone is working overtime, with no chance for R and R. This schedule will bring billable hours down, and give these folks the time off they deserve."

General Watts dropped the papers back onto his desk.

"I am authorized to bill those hours, Sergeant," he hissed through his teeth. "I am authorized to drive my people as hard as I wish. This is a top secret research facility; I am given great latitude in my position, and tremendous responsibility. If you saw one of the things I see every day, I would have to kill you. Even the head of security is not immune to the repercussions of crossing me. Do you understand me, Sergeant?"

"Sir, yes sir." He kept his sigh inward, like he had learned to do in basic training.

Watts peered up at him, narrowed his beady little eyes.

"What's your name, Sergeant?"

"Roberts, sir," he responded. "Sergeant William Roberts."

"I could write you up for this insubordination, Sergeant Roberts," Watts mused. The sergeant doubted he would; Watts was known for his inability to properly fill out or file paperwork. It was, of course, inappropriate for him to say so.

"My apologies, sir." Roberts lowered

his eyes. "I was trying to help, not hinder. I saw a way to do my job better, and give my people a chance to be rested and alert while on duty. I felt it was my duty to share."

"Your duty," General Watts sneered, "is to follow my command, not question it. Those are my people, not yours. Do you see these stars, Sergeant?"

Watts tapped his sparsely decorated lapel. Both stars look out of place, and lonely. Roberts nodded.

"They separate us by more than rank," Watts sniffed. "You've risen as high as you can, and you know why?"

"Because my parents couldn't afford to send me to officers' training like yours did for you?" Roberts postulated, aloud.

"Because I'm smarter than you," Watts corrected him. "I worked my ass off for these stars. I accomplished tasks that a man like you could only dream of. There is a reason I am the one in charge around here."

"I completely agree, sir," Roberts nodded. It was nice to be able to reply with honestly; the sergeant knew who the general's brother was. It was pretty clear to everyone, at least those who knew their congress.

"I was trying to help," Roberts reiterated. "I am in charge of security, and you are in charge of me. That is why I came to you."

"Good," Watts poked his chest again. "Remember that. I am in charge of you, and everyone here. My orders are to be regarded as law, as the word of God. Stop spending time questioning them, and focus on carrying them out."

"Sir," Roberts thought of three ways he could kill the man without moving around the desk before speaking again. "Yes, sir."

"Don't make me take you downstairs," Watts sneered. "And don't ever forget: I can make any of the people under my command disappear like that."

Watts snapped his fingers, and fell back into his chair. The sergeant saw another way to kill him, so easy and quick. It was like the man was begging for it, tempting any trained killer to take him out in his own unguarded office. Rather than point out the threat, the sergeant nodded.

"That must be quite a burden to shoulder, sir," he said, still nodding.

The general laughed; it was a cold and hollow sound.

"It's a wonderful power to wield, is what it is," he chuckled. The next word he spoke was uttered with the dripping venom that small-minded people around the world used to demean things they couldn't understand. It sounded like a slur, or an insult, though it was simply his rank.

"Sergeant," Watts spat.

He looked down at his poorly arranged desk top. Roberts had been dismissed. Rather than throttle the man, or stab or shoot him, the sergeant saluted him smartly and left the room.

*   *   *

"I'm not supposed to show you those feeds, sir,"

The man looked to his partner for support; she turned away, busied herself with knobs and dials that didn't seem to effect the screen before her at all. The sergeant ignored her; it had been clear as soon as he'd posed his question that the man was the one to press for answers.

"Do you know who I am?"

It was a question he hated, when he heard it and when he had to ask it; still, he couldn't deny that it opened doors.

"Sir," the man gulped. "Yes, sir."

"As head of all security operations, I need to see that feed."

"Of course, sir." The man glanced at his

partner's back; she was still very busy with what appeared to be a lot of nothing. He gulped again.

"It's not much, sir," he said, with a slight shrug. "More of a blur than anything."

"That blur showed up on my radar," Roberts frowned. "I need to have a good look at it before I dismiss it."

"General Watts said-"

"The general is an idiot," Roberts snapped. The woman sniggered, but didn't turn from her pointless task. "And I am in charge of security. Show me the damned blur."

"Sir," he stammered, nodding. "Yes, sir."

It really was just a blur; the sergeant had him back it up three times, play it again at normal speed.

"Freeze it there," Roberts said, the fourth time.

The image was still, a frozen blur.

"Play it forward, frame by frame," Roberts murmured.

"I have, sir. There's no-"

"Play it forward," Roberts said, lower and slower. "Frame by frame."

"Sir," the man nodded. "Yes, sir."

The woman sniggered again. Roberts ignored her, watched the monitor. His eyes narrowed as the frames advanced, then widened as the blur drifted from view.

"Go back," he snapped. "Two frames. Go back."

Roberts heard them both gasp as he frowned. The blur had stopped, for a split second, to look at the camera. It looked like a human had mated with a bear, and then died three days ago. There was an eerie intelligence in its rusted red eyes, and thick globules of blood clinging to its exposed teeth. They went back as far as he could see, rows of jagged biters that appeared to have stubborn strips of raw sinew caught between them in several places. A thick ridge rose from the top of its skull, visibly anchoring the monster's jaw across its fleshless face.

"Sergeant," the man breathed. "What is it?"

"Well, it's not a blur," Roberts pointed out. "It's not a defect in the security system either, no matter what the general said. I need you to put the facility on high alert immediately. Lock this place down. If there aren't flashing lights and warning sirens everywhere in ten seconds, I'll turn around and come back here. I'll kill you both, and set off the system myself. Understood?"

Roberts didn't wait for a reply; he stepped

into the hallway, pistol in hand. The grip was as familiar to him as his own thoughts, the weight as comforting as his own fluid mass. The sergeant moved along the wall, casting his glance quickly backward every few steps, until he reached a doorway. Lights flashed, and a siren sounded, as he pressed on past it.

The sergeant smiled, and opened the next door. He took the stairs quickly and quietly, the pistol bouncing in his hand with the natural ease of the rest of him. It had seemed like a big gun at first; when Tina had pointed out that he was a big man, and a sergeant now, he had realized that it fit perfectly in his hand. The fat grip meant more rounds, and the gun spoke to him like no other had. A week of shooting had seen him scoring higher than ever each time; after a month, he could make a bullet-sized dot disappear from the target at thirty feet. After years of searching for the perfect gun, like an artist looking for his magic brush, his wife had found it for him.

He hadn't named it; that didn't mean he didn't talk to her. Roberts muttered under his breath, the muzzle close enough to his nose to smell the oil, as he descended the stairs.

"Doesn't matter what it is," he told her.

"Only one thing matters. We're going to find it, and stop it from hurting anyone. Isn't that right, little lady?"

She didn't reply, except to continue to fit perfectly in his hand. There was already a round chambered; the sergeant considered constant readiness to be part of his job. The pistol did not have a safety; it was made for shooters that didn't have time for such things, and who did not accidentally discharge firearms. The smaller pistol in his boot was a nine with a hair trigger and two safeties; if he had time to get it out, he would have time to throw the switches and chamber a round. The fifty caliper was always ready to go from resting at his hip to distributing armor-piercing rounds in less than a second. He was unlikely to ever need the nine, or the knife in his other boot; still he strapped them on each day.

Coming out of the stairwell, the sergeant stepped into the corridor. He looked down at the tiled floor, then up at the nearest camera. Roberts tried to keep the disgust from his face; he knew they couldn't see the bloody footprints. The video feed was too grainy, and full of shadows. He considered calling out on his radio, and getting some of his best down here; for some reason he felt he was being watched, and would be listened to, by someone other than the surveillance team. He followed the bloody tracks backward, to a door marked with a clearance he didn't have.

The door was open, but not enough for him to see inside. All he was able to see from where he stood was a red wet streak on the door, the same color as the footsteps. He tried not to look too closely at the marks; if those were feet and hands that had made them, they were feet and hands like he had never seen before. Pressing his free hand against the swinging panel, Roberts felt something pressing back from the other side. He stepped back, his eyes going wide, then kicked at the door.

It swung open heavily, and a crash sounded in the room behind it. A string of fluorescents had been pulled from their moorings in the ceiling, and were flickering at odd hanging angles. The flashes of light were startling, and the sergeant backed away slowly as he shielded his eyes from the glare. He gazed into the room over the barrel of his pistol, aiming at nothing but flashing lights and dripping blood. Every surface was covered in it, caked with it, dripping blood from puddles everywhere they could have formed. Even the lights were streaked in it; white light mixed with red to cast an eerie flickering glow over everything.

The lumps of motionlessness were bodies; the sergeant realized it after staring at them for a long uncertain second. There was little left but bones, and even many of those were gone; every pile of death lay in a puddle of blood bigger than the others, and all the bones were splintered and painted in red. He could make out two skulls that had been cracked open and cleaved in half; the bloody halves were hollow, the thinking flesh scooped out to leave only blood behind.

Roberts stepped forward, kicking the door again as it tried to swing shut. Stepping into the room swiftly, he put the part of the space that he had surveyed behind him and swung the pistol smoothly with his turn. The floor was slick under his feet, and he placed each swift step carefully. As his sights lined up, he felt his breath catch in his chest. The sergeant's heart began pounding heavily in his ears, and his finger tightened on the trigger. He held it there, a reflex away from three rounds flying, as he took in the ghastly scene that was the rest of the room.

Every surface was caked in the same thick layers of red as the rest of the room; the bones were more plentiful here, and were heaped up in a bloody pile of splintered white shards. One body remained, and could be identified as human; or as half human, more accurately. His bottom half was gone, torn from his torso to pile the stack of bones higher; his top half was covered in blood, and bloody bite marks. The stub of his spine hung from his torso, and one of his arms had been chewed off at the elbow. Somehow the man was still alive; he pulled himself slowly across the slick wet tiles, his severed spine trailing through the blood.

He was slow, but strong; even with a single hand on the slick surface, he slid what was left of his body toward the sergeant with ease.

"Stop right there," Roberts breathed. "Stop or I'll shoot."

He lifted his head from his task, and met the sergeant's eyes. Roberts realized that the man was not even half human: his eyes were an unnatural rusted red, and seemed to glow eerily in the fluorescence. His skin was ashen, pale and gray; it hung from his face in lifeless chunks that looked like they were going to fall off. The only reply he gave the sergeant was a hungry hiss; Roberts saw sharp pointed teeth in the gaping maw.

There weren't rows of them, like the other creature had shown the camera; but two were enough to turn the man into a monster in his eyes. It dropped its gaze, and pulled itself another foot forward.

Roberts pulled the trigger. All three rounds struck the top of the creature's skull. It burst apart with the first shot, tossing bone and brain in a dozen directions. The next two shots turned what little was left of the skull to so much bloody pulp; as the torso struck the floor with a wet slap, it became another bloody inert pile of bones at his feet.

Following the bloody footprints, his heart pounding loudly in his ears, the sergeant moved quietly. The tracks never hesitated, or turned back; it was as if whatever had made them knew the facility as well as he did. A chill ran down his spine as he realized: many of these doors hid secrets even from him; the creature may well know the facility better. He saw the prints go into more than one room, and come back out. When they entered a room, the trail had often dwindled to a red smear or series of droplets; leaving, the full bloody footprints reappeared. The doorways were always smeared in it, and many stood ajar; the sergeant closed them quietly, and moved on each time.

It wasn't until he reached a stairwell that he paused. The sergeant was tracking two sets of prints now; at the landing, one went up while the other went down. He could hear screaming, and gunfire below. He paused on the landing, pulled the radio from his belt. With his pistol pointed down the stairs, his eyes looking up and his back against the wall, Roberts thumbed the button.

"Level three security, come back. Over."

It seemed like several minutes, waiting. It was surely only a few seconds; the sergeant forced himself to count to ten before thumbing the button again.

"Level five security, come back. Over."

He counted to twenty this time, frowned as he pressed the button one more time. "Eyes and ears, come back. Over."

"This is surveillance, sir." It was the man he had snapped orders at. "Security is down, sir."

There was a long pause.

"Sorry, sir," the man said. "Over, sir."

"What?" Roberts held the radio away from his face, as if looking at it funny would cause the man to suddenly start making sense. "What do you mean, security is down? Over."

Gunfire was coming from above and

below him now, automatic chatter punctuated by single shot reports. There was less screaming, and more of another sound that chilled him even more.

It was a hungry howl, repeated in different voices at different times. Once they all howled together, and the sergeant looked helplessly at the pistol in his hands; then the radio crackled, and surveillance came back.

'They all checked in sir," the man cried out. "We dispatched them individually, per General Watts' orders. They're gone, sir. They're all gone. Over."

"Where is the general?" Roberts asked. "Over."

"He said he was leaving, sir." The man's voice was beginning to quaver. "He told us to lift the lockdown when he got up top. Have you seen them, sir? They're everywhere, and they're monsters. They seem to know the facility, sir. They're taking over!"

Roberts held the radio away from his face again, shaking his head.

A single sheepish word sounded, broken by static. "Over."

"Is your partner still with you? Over." Roberts needed the strong smart one now; the trembling mess had served his purpose.

"Sir, yes sir." It was her voice; he relaxed

the slightest amount. "What can I do? Over."

"You can stop the general from abandoning ship," Roberts sneered. "Over."

"Already did it, sir." It sounded like she was smiling; Roberts wished it was all he could hear. There was less gunfire now, and more of those chilling howls. He brought the radio closer to his face, to hear her better.

"I called General Proctor," she went on. "I asked if it was standard policy for the commanding officer to leave a facility during lockdown. He swore a lot, sir, and said no several times in many colorful ways. Lockdown has not been compromised, sir. Over."

"Keep it short," he admonished her. "I'm in a situation. Over."

"Yes, sir," she came back. "I've got eyes; I have since you left. I'll let you know of any imminent bogies, sir. Over."

Roberts sighed. He depressed the button.

"Thanks," he breathed. He lowered his pistol, but only slightly. "How about you? What's your situation? Over."

"Sir, we are locked down," she responded, "as best we can be. These things can get through everything but plate metal, from the looks of it; and they hunt by smell, and enhanced vision. They can definitely see in the dark; in fact, they seem to prefer it. Sir, they...sorry, sir. We have several minutes before we are in danger. Over."

Roberts heard the man in the background, starting to protest before she cut the feed. The sergeant didn't have to hear him; she was being brave, but he could hear her fear. He pressed the button.

"What are they?" he asked quietly.

It was a few seconds before he realized it; the sergeant frowned, thumbed the button again. "Over."

"Don't know, sir." Her voice was brusque, clipped. "Never seen anything like it. Over."

She was trying like hell not to let her voice quaver. He waited for the howling to stop for a moment, spoke to her through the device.

"Hold tight, eyes and ears," he said. "I'm coming back up. Over."

The sergeant had climbed four stairs before the radio crackled in his hand. He turned the volume low, held it close to his ear.

"Negative, sir," she said. "The armory is right below you. Lock yourself in there. Let them come to you. Over."

Roberts paused between steps. He pressed the button.

"I have a fifty caliper pistol," he said proudly. "I have three clips, twenty-eight rounds remaining. I can get to you. Over."

"No, sir," she came back. Her voice wasn't clipped any more; it was trembling, and breaking. He could hear savage thuds behind her words. "I lied to you before, sir. They're coming through now. It's not just a few, sir. They're changing the troops, sir. They're becoming monsters, and hunting down the others. You need to get to the armory, sir. They could already be there. They seem to retain some memories after they change. They change by eating people, sir. Try shooting them in the eye, sir. Good luck, sir. Eyes and ears, over and out."

The last thing he heard was a final crash, and the man crying out. Roberts reversed his course and took the stairs two at a time. He heard the door crash open below, and slowed his pace. Backing against the wall, he rounded the corner and squinted along his sights. It was a monster all right; it also clearly had a skull. Roberts shot it, twice.

Its head rocked backward with each report. Roberts saw the gashes open in its forehead, on either side of the thick bony ridge that started high on its brow. Watching the creature calmly, he saw the gashes close as if they had never been. It looked at him, as if daring the sergeant to do better. Shifting slightly, Roberts heard her voice in his mind.

"Try shooting them in the eye, sir."

Its rusted red left eye was his whole world for a fraction of a second. Roberts squeezed the trigger, the eye exploded in a burst of blood, and the creature crumpled to the floor. He descended the stairs, kicked at the inert form, peeked around the corner. There were more, too many to count. He waited until one of them turned, and came for him; the pistol erupted in his hand, and the red orb turned into a red splatter. The monster fell to the floor, thirty feet from him.

Two more were coming at him before it hit the tile; Roberts dropped one, and backed into the stairwell. Dashing up steps two at a time, he turned as the next creature filled the landing. Bullets flew as he took aim, the gun bucking in his grip. They ripped two wide holes in the monster's chest, and gave it pause; but the holes didn't bleed, and the creature kept on coming. Roberts took out its right eye, then tried to shoot the left before it fell. The action on his pistol stood open, the clip empty.

One hand held the gun in place, his eyes still along the sights. The other stuck the empty clip in his pocket, swapped it for a full one. It only took a second, maybe two; he had practiced the motion until there were no pauses or hesitation. It was all the time they needed to fill the entry, and begin to ascend the stairs; the next four shots were placed with care, and four monsters fell. The fifth paused, startled as they fell; he came at the sergeant, and Roberts carefully placed another shot.

Stepping gingerly over the bodies, he peeked into the hallway again. He could see the armory from here, and no monsters. That didn't make sense; they should have been going for the biggest cache of the largest weapons onsite. He paused a few interminable moments, wondering if it was a trap; then he remembered.

A few weeks ago a new system had been installed; critical systems had been wired into an override feed offsite. The armory was locked down, against him and the monsters. Roberts turned and dashed up the stairs, his boots pounding loudly against every other step. Rounding the corners carefully, he climbed past the next two flights as fast as he could. The last corner was a cluster of monsters, blocking his path. He counted silently as he fired rounds their way. The last two caught the lead monster, as it ducked under the lethal spray to come at the sergeant on all fours.

There was another pile of bodies to walk over, as his last clip slid into place. The sergeant chambered a round, lifting his foot over the bloody mess. Something hissed, and writhed, and suddenly the sergeant was falling. He landed in the midst of the monsters, and felt one of them moving against him; he heard the pistol clatter on the floor. In a startling instant it gained its feet, and held him aloft. The fingers around his throat felt like vices, and the talons scraped the back of his head like razors. Roberts felt a dozen tiny slices opening up on the back of his head, as the creature positioned its mighty claws.

Roberts pulled his knee up, felt the razored sharpness dig deeper. There was distance between them, and the monster brought back its other arm to swipe his skull from his shoulders. The nine made a clicking and clacking sound as Roberts chambered a round; he shoved the barrel in the creature's gaping maw and squeezed until it dropped him. It staggered backward as he dove for his other pistol, a puff of smoke rising from its mouth. It was on him again the moment

Roberts turned away, opening its mouth to take a piece of his leg.

One bullet finally found its eye; the orb exploded, but the monster did not go down. It shook it off, threw back its head and howled. The sergeant dropped the nine, put both hands on the other pistol grip. When the other eye was leveled at him, he squeezed the familiar trigger. There was a burst of blood, and the monster went down.

"Ten," he muttered, kneeling to holster the nine again. He noticed that his hands and fatigues were splashed and streaked in blood. A tentative hand at the back of his head came away wet, and he felt a warm trickle down his spine. He stepped over the bodies again, putting his foot down in a growing puddle of slick red. Every other footprint was a bloody one as he pushed through the door.

"Nine," the sergeant said, calmly.

The creature turned. Its eye exploded, and it stood there uncertain for a moment; then it fell heavily to the floor. Two more came at him, from either side of the one falling, and he called out as the bullets flew.

"Eight, seven, six." He couldn't hear his own voice anymore; there was nothing but dull ringing in his ears, the pounding of his heart and the muffled reports as he fired.

They fell, to be replaced by two more.

"Five, four," the sergeant cried, backing away as he fired.

One creature dropped, the other lunged at him. Roberts was pressed against the floor, the air whooshing out of him as the pistol clattered away once more. He punched and kicked, dodged a mouthful of teeth and rolled toward the pistol. Lying sideways, he murmured into a puddle of blood.

"Three," he frowned. "Two."

It was on top of him, bleeding from both eye sockets; the body was still twitching, but it was dead. He shoved it off, glanced to make sure the slide was not standing open. Roberts lurched to his feet, spit out a bloody tooth and moved swiftly to his office. The door was ajar, and swung open at his touch; the moment the creature looked up at him, the sergeant put it down. Dropping to one knee, he had the nine in his hand before he got a good view of the rest of the room.

It was empty, save for the body bleeding from one eye. Roberts moved behind his desk, set the spent weapon on the sparse surface. Digging his keys from a pocket in his fatigues, he knelt beside the square bottom drawer. The nine millimeter stayed in his hand, resting on the desk and pointing at the open doorway. Drawer open, Roberts removed two boxes of fifty caliper hollow point rounds. He put one on the desk and the other beside him on the floor, and frantically began to reload the clips from his other pocket. One was full, the next nearly full, when he heard the steady sound of bestial footfalls; there were at least two, or one coming on all fours. The sound was a thud in time with a scraping squeal, in rapid sets of four.

Sliding one full clip home and stashing another in his pocket, the sergeant left the third clip on the desk next to the nine. He saw the creature blur by the open doorway, catching the jamb with one set of claws; Roberts stood up, and took aim. It skidded on the tile for a full second, like a ghastly cartoon. As soon as its head came around the corner he relieved it of one eye; the creature froze for a moment, so Roberts took the other as well. There were two more behind it, approaching carefully around the corpse. As soon as their heads came into view, Roberts rattled their skulls with bullets. One pulled back; the other fell to join the first.

He snatched the empty clip, crouched behind the desk again, started stuffing rounds into it. It was slower with one hand, but this was the reason he had practiced the task; when the monster peered around the corner, he squeezed off two more shots. It staggered, but didn't fall. Two more shots, and it stopped staggering; one of its eyes exploded in its socket, and the thing dropped to the floor. The slide stood open on the pistol.

"Well, hell," he muttered, dropping the clip and slamming home another. There were no sounds, and Roberts moved as fast as he could to get the clips filled once more. He never quite got around to completing his task. He wouldn't know until later, when they told him, that he was locked down in his office for over forty-eight hours. They watched, on a live feed, as he took out every member of what used to be the facility's personnel. There were tanks outside, and a score of armed helicopters overhead; they never saw anything but a locked down building. To them it seemed like days, days spent away from home.

To him it felt like a few hours; at one point he wondered if he would ever hear right again, and how many spent shells were gathering at his feet; then he shrugged, and began sweeping the rolling brass toward the door with his feet.

It saved him when the general tried to rush in; it was done with the typical brash arrogance with which the man did everything. He got a good running start from across the hallway, and hit the opening at a good clip; he was even smart enough to keep his head down. Roberts noticed the stars, watched his eyes come up and go wide when the brass rolled under his feet; both rusted red orbs were bleeding by the time he stuck the desk with his thick skull.

The rest were a blur, save a few members of his security team. It was no harder to put them down than it had been easy to take out the general; looking in their eyes before shooting them out, Roberts saw no trace of humanity in their hungry fevered gazes. He had never questioned his decision to stockpile so much ammunition for one gun; he resolved more than once that the pile would be bigger next time, if he made it out of this alive. The thought came every time he reached in for a couple more boxes of rounds; there was one grenade in there, and he had reached for it more than once. Whatever these things were, he was not becoming one of them.

When they stopped coming, someone shut off the lights and sirens. A unit came in with bulletproof shield, and the sergeant nearly emptied a clip into one of them; then he spied the face behind it, and collapsed into a pile of shells. They jangled merrily against his face, and Roberts resisted the urge to laugh along with them. He let the team help him up, and get him on a stretcher, before he finally relaxed his hold on consciousness.

*       *       *

"I don't understand," Tina took his hand on the table, squeezed gently. "I thought you couldn't get promoted any more."

Roberts was in a haze, but at least he was home. Some very important people had come to talk to him while he was being evaluated; he had only been allowed a brief call home, to tell her he was fine and that it would be awhile longer. Tina hadn't raised or lowered her voice; she had simply told him she was glad everything was fine, and she couldn't wait to see him. It was three days before they were sitting together at the dining room table, holding hands and talking.

'There were special circumstances," he shrugged. "Top secret circumstances. I can tell you a little about it, if you like."

"I saw the tanks," she squeezed his hand again. "I saw the helicopters, and the families packing up in the last few days. If it's top secret, I only want to know one thing: do you want it?"

"It would be dangerous," he squeezed back. "More routine, like this security detail was, but as risky as the old days."

"You said the old days wouldn't have been half as risky if you'd had your fifty caliper." Tina smiled. "Don't forget her."

"I haven't." He held her eyes, to let her know he was serious. "It will be as risky as the old days."

"Okay." Tina drew the word out slowly, lifting her other hand to the table as well. Both of them together barely covered his single meaty hand.

"You know," she pointed out, "you still haven't answered me. I don't want to have images of what may be endangering you unless you will feel better having me know about it. I know what you do. I know that if you turn this down, someone else will get it; it's hard to imagine that person being more qualified than you. They came to you because you deserve it, and your country needs you; all of that is abundantly clear. What I need to know right now is the same thing you need to ask yourself. Do you want it?"

He nodded; he had thought it over as well, and couldn't disagree with any of her points. He met her eyes, looked into them and nodded again.

"I do," Roberts said. "If you're okay with it, I want it."

Tina leaned forward; he met her halfway across the table, closed his eyes as her lips pressed against his. They lingered that way for a wonderful moment, long enough for him to remember that he had considered never feeling it again a few short days ago. When she pulled away there were tears in his eyes, and her beauty swam in and out of focus until he blinked it away.

"Well, General," she said, for the first time. "You had better go claim those stars, and find out where we'll be moving to next. I'll get packing."

They stood at the same time, and he gathered her up in his arms.

"I couldn't do this without you," he murmured. "I need you now more than ever. You're the reason I'm still alive, in every way."

"I know," she breathed, her words nearly lost in his chest. "Good thing I'm not going anywhere. I need you too, you know."

He held her closer, buried his face in her hair.

# PROLOGUE PREQUEL EPILOGUE

"What's your first name, Sergeant?"

"Sir?" the man gave Roberts a curious look. "Leo, sir."

The general stuck his hand out across his desk.

"I'm Bill," he said. "It's nice to meet you, Leo."

He hesitated; the general had known he would. Their first week together had been a blur for Roberts; the only time he had paid attention to his head of security was at night, when he went through the grainy tapes. The man never smiled, or frowned; his serious mien had been the first thing to strike the general. It hadn't been the last.

Finally, he reached out and shook the general's hand.

He spoke, as they felt each other's grips.

"It's not necessary to-"

"Normally," the general cut him off, let his hand go. "I would agree. These are the most special circumstances I have been witness to, and I have seen some things. I chose you myself, and I have been watching you carefully. Your file doesn't tell the whole story on you, but I have learned enough. I have requested special clearance for you and you alone. You need to know what we're dealing with here."

The general motioned for him to sit; again, the man hesitated. Roberts waited, and settled in after the sergeant.

"Leo," he said, then stopped. "May I call you Leo?"

"Sir," Leo nodded. "Yes, sir."

Roberts smiled. "Leo, I was in your shoes not long ago. The general in charge of the facility I was stationed at was an idiot. He made it very difficult to do our jobs, and when we needed to do them most we failed. He didn't tell me what I'm about to tell you; if he had, it may well have saved hundreds of lives. Up until a few weeks ago, I worked with over five hundred people. They are all dead now, except for me. I need you to know what I did not know, so you can do a better job than I did."

The sergeant looked at him, expressionless.

"I've seen your file, of course," Roberts said. "I've also watched you shoot, and handle people. You are a better shot than I am, and you live to make everything work for everyone you lead. That means you're probably a better leader than I am as well. If you like to drink anything in particular, please let me know what it is. I have much to learn from you; I feel that the closer we work together, the better our chances of saving the people under our command. They are beginning work downstairs, and I would like to take you down there to see for yourself."

"General," Leo said, his face still expressionless, "I'm quite sure I will believe you if you tell me."

The general nodded.

"I don't doubt that," Roberts replied. "Don't feel bad if you change your mind partway through the telling. The facility I used to work at did all kinds of experiments, and one day one of them got loose. It was a patient, a human patient, who had transformed into something quite inhuman. It was taller, and stronger, and faster; it ate everyone in the lab, then got loose in the facility. When it didn't eat someone all the way, that person became a monster as well. Most of the people I used to work with were eaten by each other; the rest of them became flesh-eating monsters, and tried to eat me. I killed them all. Will you help me stop that from happening again?"

Leo didn't speak for nearly a minute. The general let him take his time, watched the frozen mask that was his face.

"I was given quarters," he said, finally. "They are on the other side of the base. I would like to be quartered here; if it's all the same to you, sir."

Roberts shook his head, smiled slightly.

"It's not all the same," he replied. "I appreciate it."

"Thank you, sir," the sergeant said. "I was also given an office. It's on a different floor than this one. If I may, sir..."

"We'll set you up next door," Roberts nodded. "We'll cut a door in the wall between if you want."

The sergeant looked as though he was about to smile for a moment; he visibly resisted the urge.

"Next door would be fine, sir." He rose. "I'd like to go pack my things, sir."

"Of course," Roberts stood as well. "I'll call facilities and have them set you up with living quarters. They'll be all that you have now, if not more. You'll also see a bump in pay, if you'll be turning down housing."

"I don't need much room, sir," Leo said.

"Or a bump in pay."

The general shrugged. "You'll get it, just the same."

Roberts extended his hand again. There was no hesitation this time; the sergeant grasped it, shook his hand firmly and dropped it. He turned, and the general watched him leave. At the door he hesitated.

"Scotch, sir," the sergeant opened the door, stepped out as he spoke. "I like scotch, sir."

Roberts let a broad smile come across his face as the door clicked closed behind the sergeant. He checked the middle drawer of his desk, made sure the bottle was mostly full, closed the drawer again.

Before his mind could drift forward to the next most horrific experience of his life, a light flashed on his desk. That would be Tina. He smiled, popped the last bit of meatloaf in his mouth and pressed the button that would patch her through.

# ABOUT JOHN'S STONES

Was that fun? I hope you loved it. I can honestly say that I never thought I would write a 'prologue prequel epilogue'. Now I'm glad to say that I have; and it just happened naturally!

Meditation seems to come up in all of my projects at some point. I caught Somebody meditating in 'Stumbling Backasswards Into the Light'; there was a meditating dragon in the 'Walking Between Worlds' books; and now I've moved on to zombie meditation. Let me elaborate a little here, in case you haven't read the book. If you have, allow me to elaborate anyway; it can be easier outside of the context of the story, sometimes.

The monsters in 'Zombie Zero' share a hive mind. Although individuals, their consciousness is a collective one; they even have a queen! Their hunger unites them, as does the grisly mission they are here to complete. With their minds linked together like this, they are able to cooperate in some chilling ways. Their old desires are gone, but their minds remain as sharp as ever.

The mental power that they spread so thin as humans has found razor keen awareness within their new monstrous shapes, and that awareness is a collective one.

Focus is one of the most interesting subjects in the world to me. I was a fairly young kid when I first noticed that many of my favorite stories had a common theme to them: some main character or characters would go from a slow-paced normal existence to a frantic focused search for something or someone. I remember thinking more than once: why not just go get that thing when life was easy? Why wait until everything starts to fall apart before making a gargantuan effort to get it together?

The answers seem simple now: first, normal life has a lot of things you have to pay attention to if you want to live it well. Second, it's not desire that drives most of us into that frantic searching state: it's need.

This is the story of a man who became a monster, then remembered what had made him a man before. He finds a unique way to combine the two, as he searches desperately for an answer to the zombie outbreak problem. This story happens somewhere between Chapter 17 and Chapter 21 in 'Zombie Zero: The First Zombie'.

# JOHN'S STONES

His beastly new body seemed perfectly suited for meditation. John's long legs crossed easily into the lotus posture, with none of the usual strain on his hips or knees. His iron spine locked into place naturally, and his mind cleared instantly. There was no need for his old mantra, or deliberate measured breathing; his mind opened up as soon as he closed his eyes, and he saw the whole world. It was a vast network, the hive mind of the monsters; but there were pieces missing, one in particular.

John looked closer, honing in on the area by language. Australia was already full of them; he could see nearly any inhabited city on the entire continent. Europe would fall in the next wave; but America should be his to explore mentally. He scanned, and found a pocket of them. John zeroed in on one, inhabited his mind.

Panic flooded him, and hunger. He knew everything all at once, and felt it: this was a secure room, and it was filled with howlers. John could feel their hunger, and smell their panic. He dove deeper into the monster's mind, searching for the source of their fear.

A shudder passed through him. Before this man had become a zombie, he had already been a monster. It didn't take much digging to see what he had done, and how long he had been behind bars for it. They had come for him, told him that it was time for the death penalty, and injected him. When he woke up, the room was full of other prisoners; soon it was nothing but blood and howlers. After they had eaten what could be eaten, they had linked minds and tried to escape; an hour later they wandered the room together, hungry and frightened.

The room reeked of death. It had only been him and a room full of flesh at first; then the powerful scent of hot splashing blood had overwhelmed him as he fed. It wasn't until after they ran out of flesh that they had noticed the odor of old death lingering under the new. That death smelled like them, like howlers. It had driven them into the shared panic that awaited whatever had put them in here, whatever was coming for them. Howlers had been in this room before; they had left it in bags, and their blood still stained the walls red.

John watched through his eyes, calmed

the monster's thoughts with his own. He reminded the creature that there was a higher purpose to what he had become, and coaxed him into calming his breathing. When the smell of flesh filled the room once more, the other monsters made for the smell; John's hung back, kept to the wall, and circled around slowly. He heard a voice calling out, giving shouted instructions.

"Keep your backs to each other!" she yelled. Her voice was both calm and strident, confident and tremulous at the same time. "Keep them back with your rifles, and then press forward when they fall!"

A burst of automatic gunfire erupted, and howls rent the air. The wet thick sound of metal striking bone came to his host's ears again and again, and the monster tried to bolt from his hold. John held him, traced his way along the wall until he came up behind the carefully structured formation. They faced out in all directions, and every other one of them was covered from head to toe in some kind of exoskeleton armor. The rest were in fatigues, and they were the only aggressors. They fired their weapons at the howlers in front of them; when one would fall, the phalanx would provide cover fire while one of them moved in. John saw the flash of blue steel several times, and watched a howler's head roll.

When he saw an opening, John pressed the creature into action. He overrode his host's instincts, and leapt nearly straight up to fall neatly inside the circle. The floor struck the monster's feet, and John forced him to fall to the hard tiling. He bit at an uncovered ankle, then slashed away the jagged scraps of skin with his talons. There was only time for one more set of gashes before the formation spread out, and separated the host's head from his body. John felt his own mind snap back like a rubber band, and he opened his eyes with an involuntary cry.

Closing his eyes, John reached out again with his mind. He leapt from one monster's mind to the next, nimbly, as the unit took them out one by one. He watched the man he had bitten, pressing on against the pain and resisting the change. John saw an opening, and went through it.

He was human again. John looked out through the weak ordinary eyes, wrapped his thoughts around the man's groping mind. The man wondered if he had been bitten; John assured him it was only a scratch, with the calming sound of the man's own inner voice. He wondered if a scratch could turn him, despite what they said; John soothed him with whispered promises. Then John heard him wondering where the voice in his head was coming from, and he dominated the man's mind completely. The weak awkward movements of humanity were his to wield once more.

John stumbled, and one of the exoskeletons caught him.

"I've got you," he said. His voice was distorted slightly by the mask, or the speaker system in the suit. The hands that held him up were unnaturally strong, and bore most of his sagging bulk easily.

"I'm okay," John muttered, leaning his weight back onto the weak and shaky noodles that should have been his legs.

The helmet shifted, looking down at the wound. John couldn't see his face through the reflective surface; he heard him let out a low whistle.

"Looks like you got sliced up pretty good," he said, leaning in closer. "No bite marks, though. I know it might not feel like it, but you got off easy. Hang back while we sweep the room, and we'll get you to medical."

John didn't realize how much he had been leaning on the suit until he walked away. He wobbled for a moment, then sat down awkwardly on the floor. Putting his head between his knees, he held tight to his thoughts. He pushed away the effects of the bite, talking to the change as if it were a person he could reason with.

'Just a little more time,' he told it, 'a little longer appearing human, and then I'll feed you.'

When he felt a tap on his shoulder, John looked up. He smiled weakly, and took the hand that was proffered him.

"You look pretty pasty, friend," the distorted voice told him. "You sure you didn't get bit?"

John hesitated, leaning his weight on the suit.

"Look at that puddle of blood, Smiley," another suit of armor said, coming up behind them. "Of course he's pasty; you left the poor guy there to bleed out."

She knelt at his side, tore off one of his pant legs and wrapped it snug around the wound. Standing up, she put her shoulder under his other arm and hefted the rest of his weight easily. John went back to breathing like a human should, convincing his body that it was only a flesh wound. It took everything he had; he began to doze off while he lay there being bandaged, and felt his own distant consciousness try to pull him back. When they told him to rest, he insisted that he would rest better at home; after a brief debate, the doctor threw up her hands. She gave him some dressings, and specific instructions to call base medical if there were any complications.

John dragged the body to its locker, then to its car. He slumped in the driver's seat, and barely managed to return the friendly wave at the security checkpoint. It took nearly five minutes of driving before he saw an exit with tall signs boasting national retail chain outlets. The change was taking hold now; they looked like flesh ads to his twisted hunger. John got off on the ramp, coasted right up to the sidewalk in front of a storefront, and set the parking brake. He had barely pulled himself from the car with agonizing slowness when a man approached him.

"Sir," he said, "you can't park there."

John lifted his head, slowly, to meet his eyes.

"Sir, are you alri-"

John fell forward, and the man caught him. He tried to heft John's weight, shifting his arm to grasp more firmly. John caught the arm as it passed, sinking his teeth into the man's meaty forearm. Blood flooded his mouth, along with the taste of flesh and hair and sleeve. The man cried out, but only briefly; as John felt his mind come back to him, and the body transform, the man pressed his arm into John's mouth insistently. He fed, consuming the arm up to the shoulder as his teeth grew in. As he sunk rows of new jagged biters into the man's neck, a voice called out behind them.

"Hey!" He sounded scared, or angry. "Get off him! What are you doing? Hey!"

John lifted his head, pulling at the mouthful of flesh until it tore free in a burst of blood. He turned, swallowed, and howled.

The man that had called out backed up a step involuntarily, then stood there trembling. John watched a dark wet stain appear on his slacks, and he howled again. Turning from the spoiled meat, he spied a pretty morsel that smelled like pears. John smiled; he liked pears. He ate most of her face before she could use it to scream, and stripped her to bones in the space of a minute. His temporary body thrilled at the sustenance; John felt warm lively tingles in his limbs as they grew longer and stronger. He held on to the monster's mind until he had bitten a dozen others, then slipped back into his own powerful form.

John opened his eyes. Leaping to his feet, he threw his head back and howled. He passed the three terrified troops chained to his desk without a glance, and went out into the night that had fallen on his side of the world. John hunted with a clear mind, and hope; it had begun, even there. The fact that he still couldn't reach the one mind he had been searching for was not a concern for him any longer; his mind was consumed with his hunger, and his new knowledge of a trained team of zombie killers. He'd have to tell Maya about that, after he ate.

*   *   *

The next time he dipped his mind into the buzzing hive, John sent more howlers to the base. Then he reached out, and found the others that had changed. It wasn't long before he found himself several stories underground, inhabiting the sodden mind of a rambler. He was strapped to a table, consumed by hunger, and aware of what he was. A man was talking to him, almost too fast for John to keep up.

"Doctor, can you hear me?" he asked.

"Can you speak?"

Several people were looking at him; many of them were looks of concern. One woman leaned forward, frowned.

"I told you this was a bad idea," she said.

John could smell her, through his host's nose; he tried to sit up, and taste her. The restraints protested, but they held him.

"He has to change again," another voice cried out.

She came forward, shouldered the older woman out of her way.

"He has to feed, and then change," she insisted. "Then he can communicate with us. I'll do it."

She unbuttoned her cuff, began to roll up her shirt. John felt a twisting pain in the heart that belonged to the mind he had occupied; he cared for her. The twisting continued as she went on.

"He believes in this cure," she said. "So do I. Let him feed on me a little, talk to him, and then give us both his new cure. Then give us both the vaccination and try to turn us again."

"That won't be necessary," the older woman shook her head. "We have a more suitable candidate for assisting in the rest of Doctor Cho's transformation. Don't we,

Doctor Regis?"

They all continued to stare at him; after a moment, one of them started, stood up straighter.

"Yes," he nodded, still watching John's host. "Yes, we do."

The woman sighed, nodded to the nearest person with a large automatic rifle in his hands.

"Bring in the volunteer," she said.

"Someone volunteered?" the younger woman asked, puzzled.

The man was already being brought in, chains binding his wrists together and securing them to his belted waist.

"Some people raise their hands and step up," she replied. "Others commit horrible crimes against the people we are sworn to protect, and we tend to take that as a pretty clear message. If we can catch them, we can do whatever we wish with them."

She nodded to the pair escorting the prisoner, stepped back.

"Back up, everyone," she advised them. "The doctor's legs will still be restrained, but they're going to let his arms loose. Would you two please secure the volunteer to the doctor's bed railing, and let loose his upper body restraints? Don't stop him when he gets started; let him have his fill. We want him to transform completely if possible."

The prisoner's eyes went wider with each word she spoke; he tried to resist his captors. The man on his left seized him by the wrist and shoulder, while the woman on his right kicked the back of his knee and caught the rest of his weight. Together they dragged him to the railing, and secured him to it. They stepped back, and hefted their weapons.

John looked around. He saw the man watching him, and all the others. There was more than one rifle trained on him. His hunger twisted at his belly, and he let the host body grab the trembling prisoner. He watched through his rusted red eyes while the change came over another monster, saw the doctor's thoughts come back to him while blood soaked his face and flesh filled his belly.

"Oh, good God," the doctor sputtered. John tried to watch his thoughts, follow the quicksilver stream of the new monster's mind.

"I'm connected to all of them," his host growled. "One of them is in my head right now, trying to stop me from telling you this. They know where we are. They-"

John filled the man's mind with a searing spear of light. He cried out, his hunger twisting his brain to a new paradigm. When John vacated the doctor's consciousness, he knew more than he had hoped for. He knew everything he had been trying to learn. John knew where she was. He left the fried circuits behind, snapped back to his own monstrous form. It was time to feed until he'd had his fill, and go see Maya.

* * *

She was the heart of the monsters, the prime directive woven deeply into the fabric of the hive mind. All that they knew, she knew; all they could do, they would do for her. She was Maya, irresistible and terrible and beautiful. Her orders were to find Elayna, to bring his daughter back into the fold. John felt Maya watching from behind his eyes while they crossed the ocean. She showed him the layout of the facility, and the neighborhood around it. Inside the facility, she twisted one young woman's sickness into the first signs of hunger. She gave into it as he neared the location on foot; suddenly, John had eyes in the facility.

He directed the pilot that had flown him

here to feed, and took to hunting his own series of fresh bites of flesh. In minutes they had surrounded the underground base with howlers, hundreds that turned to thousands as they fed. When the team of armored agents came for them, they were ready. The zombies closed in on them, hemming them in slowly. Two of the enemy broke loose together, and John called a dozen howlers to his side. They hunted the duo until one stepped away from the other; it was all they needed.

John was in an alley, waiting for the blur that deposited his victim before him. He'd been struck so hard that it had knocked him unconscious; the pilot must have been streaking along at nearly sixty miles per hour. The sound of a blade striking bone sounded nearby, several times; John called out to them to fall back, in his mind. He had what he needed. The man's security badge was affixed to his waist; John pried it loose and began to walk away. John motioned to the pilot, and he followed.

Steel sang behind them, a sword being freed of its scabbard. The exoskeleton had regained its consciousness, and its feet. John shook his head at his companion, called out to the others. A hungry crowd closed in as they drew back, and the sounds of melee faded behind them. A powerful explosion blew out the alley they had been fighting in, and most of the street beyond, as he burst into the office building at the center of the constricting circle of howlers. Without looking back, he made his way to the rear bank of elevators. The other monster followed silently.

The set of sliding doors looked like the other three; he held the dead man's badge up to the call button. It lit up, and the steel moved aside. As the doors closed behind them, an emotionless voice sounded above.

"Authorization access code required," the voice prompted. "Please state access code to proceed."

John whirled, tried to pry at the doors. His talons could not slide through the seam, or split the steel. Turning again, he saw nothing but thick welded metal plates on all sides. His companion watched him, waited for an order.

"State your authorization code immediately," the voice insisted emotionlessly. "Elevator will lock down in nine...eight..."

John fell to the floor, tore the carpet and pad to shreds as his claws scraped loudly against the metal below it. It took him a full two seconds to find a seam, another three to stomp it enough times to blow a hole in the floor. Once it came loose enough to get his hands in there, John peeled the floor away like an aluminum can. The other creature dropped to its knees, pulled at the other side. He leapt straight up, hugged his arms to his sides, and dropped through the hole; John was right behind him. The imitation human voice finished the countdown as his head cleared the hole; a thick green gas began to fill the box, and a second slab of steel slid to cover the hole they had made.

A high-pitched siren sounded, a muffled disembodied voice announced a security breach. He heard it as he fell, the hallways beyond being filled with the warning.

Something struck him before his flailing arms could find purchase. John careened off it, and got tangled painfully in a network of steel cabling. He extricated himself, and lowered his body along one of the cables. When he knew that he was deep within the facility, he pried at a set of outer doors; they opened easily, whooshing into the wall once he had pulled them apart a few inches. In the hallway he paused, orienting himself Maya's network of minds.

A set of razored talons reached through the opening, and then another. The other monster pulled himself up and into the corridor wordlessly. He straightened, stood next to John and waited.

"The new cure is on this floor," John told him. "They have developed an inoculation as well. Destroy all of the labs, all of the medicine and all of the research. Leave no stone unturned and no human unchanged. You go that way. I'll meet you back here."

John let his thoughts run wild as he turned and made his way away from the pilot. He heard crashing and screaming behind him as he kicked in the first door he came to; it was empty, a break room of some kind. Glancing back over his shoulder, burying his actions under layers of meaningless thought, he passed several other doors. The one he finally kicked in was full of people in lab coats, beakers and scales and glass measuring containers. And pills. He tore through the people, shattered every piece of glass, and stuffed his pockets with pills. The motion was done as mindlessly as possible, while he focused his thoughts on the biting and breaking. A fire broke out while he fed, and John moved to the next room.

Every space that had anything worth

destroying in it was a shattered mess within minutes; several of the rooms were on fire, and thick noxious smoke streamed into the hallway. John found the pilot, led him to the stairwell. They pounded down the flights together wordlessly, unchallenged. The closer he got, the more he could feel her again. By the time they reached the floor she was on, John could hear her heart beating in his ears. Bursting through the first door, he heard it more clearly; only a hallway and another door stood between them now. The badge he was still carrying opened it, and they approached her while she dozed.

John watched her, letting the love fill his heart. He hoped it would cloak the thoughts in his mind just a little longer. Maya couldn't have possibly seen his deeper desire in all of this; she never would have sent him. The pilot couldn't know either, until it was too late. He watched her sleep for a few precious moments, spoke as softly as his monstrous new voice would allow.

"Elayna," John called out.

She didn't stir. The howler next to him made as if to step forward; John let a heavy hand of warning fall on his shoulder. He shook his head, spoke again.

"Elayna," he said, louder.

This time she moved, lifting her head from the pillow and blinking sleepy eyes at him.

"Elayna, sweetie, we have to go," John murmured.

Her face was still relaxed in sleep, her eyes unfocused and unseeing; her flesh had begun to grow back, and a thin layer of hair covered her head. Altogether it made for a gruesome sight to anyone but him: John saw her as a baby, as a little girl just waking up, as an adult that had become his friend, and as the only one of them that had resisted the twisting gnawing hunger for human flesh. There was no possible way for him to love or admire a human being more than he did her in that moment, no matter his monster's heart. When she spoke it broke the dam within him, and his thoughts poured forth.

"Daddy?" Her voice was almost completely her own again. It was sweet music to his ears, and he let his face break out in a ghastly grin. John knew Maya was watching him: he let her see, dared her to try and stop him. He let her watch him talk to her, and rip the head off the pilot when he suggested that Elayna needed to feed. As the monster's blood spattered his face, John felt a shift within him.

The presence was gone. The buzzing hive remained, like a mist he could reach out and touch; otherwise he was alone in his mind for the first time since Maya had twisted it. He was still hungry, but it wasn't her hunger anymore. John felt his soul sing with the freedom, and his own thoughts come flooding back to his monstrous brain. His first thought was getting Elayna somewhere safe; there was a nice brick brownstone nearby that would do just fine. After that, he would do all he could to right the wrong he had committed.

John might not be able to save the world, or the millions already lost; but he was going to do whatever he could. The thoughts that he couldn't push away, as he formulated his plan, would plague him persistently until his mind found its way out of the clustered network of wet tissue that currently housed it. Could this have been what Maya had planned from the very beginning? Was this why the five of them had been chosen, to both start and stop this bloody series of tragedies? Was everything that he was doing the same thing that had been done before, and would be done again? Was he throwing stones at the wind, trying to make it stop blowing?

# ABOUT TINA'S BEDSIDE

Throw those stones, John. I'm rooting for you. Was that a fun take on the power of meditation? If zombies are possible, I don't see why a good ol' mind zap shouldn't be as well. You'll see more of what John is up to in this next story, and a little more of what he can do with that sharp zombie mind of his. That's not all this story is about, though...

Rather than spoil what you are about to read in any way, I would rather give you my emotional impressions of the story. First, I should preface those impressions with some context. See, I'm a pretty emotional guy. I really connect with these characters, as deeply in many ways as I connect with the people I love on this side of the page. It can be hard to watch them go through their trials, or be consumed by their demons.

Yet I can't change what I see through the magical lens in my mind. I've tried, and the story won't have it; it stops speaking to me, I stop seeing those precious images, and I can't go on until I've written it as it's being told to me.

So I act as observer, and scribe, and tell the stories as best I can. I see myself as a campfire storyteller gone digital and print; with the popularity of campfires dramatically down, it seemed a wise choice. It also gives me the opportunity to edit before presenting, and tell the story right the first time; old storytellers honed their craft like modern comics, tweaking the tale with each telling until it was just right. You don't have to see the awkward first draft, or any of the subsequent ones; you get the best version the first time!

(And I don't have to worry about my long hair being singed by campfires.)

The thing you don't get with this medium is my emotional reactions to telling it. It's probably for the best; you might respect me less if you saw how many tears actually fall. As a somewhat helpless observer, I watch these lives with nearly the same intensity that I engage in my own.

And in my life, I cry when I'm happy. I cry when I'm sad. I cry when something moves me, or touches me deeply. I probably cried at some point writing each of these stories; this one really turned on the waterworks, and I was grateful for every tear.

I hope you enjoy 'Tina's Bedside'.

# TINA'S BEDSIDE

The general heard the quiet tone repeat itself. He waited calmly, as if he hadn't already tried twelve numbers without success. At least this time it was ringing, instead of going to a recording telling him that this was not a valid number. He listened to the soft pulse again, and waited calmly for the next. It never came. The line was open; there was no greeting, just an open line.

"Special Agent," he said. "This is General Roberts. A certain device in my office has been acting very strangely. I am sure you know why. Unless I am mistaken, I need some people to train my troops. Can you provide me with some...specialists?"

He knew whose voice he was about to hear; what he didn't know was that a flood of memories would come rushing back at the sound of it. The words were delivered simply, without an excess or absence of emotion; they were few, brief and to the point. The general responded in kind.

"Twenty, at least," he said. "Fifty would be better."

Again, he listened for the response; again, it made him remember the last time he had heard that voice. Even when it shouted orders, it was calm and cool; even when it faced what appeared to be certain death, that voice did not waver. The sound of it brought scenes of stacked corpses, burning and rising from the flames; of both men back to back, him screaming and the other calmly responding, while one flaming monster after another fell at their feet. It was strange how so few words could bring back so many memories.

"Well, then," the general frowned. "How many can you send?"

His frown deepened at the response. He discarded the hard exterior he wore for a moment, there in the relative privacy of his office. Both lines were secure, which meant at least two people were listening in; the general didn't care.

"That's goddamned ridiculous," he snapped. "You and I have been charged with mounting a last line of defense in this situation. My resources and funding have dwindled and been diverted over the years to put me in a very difficult position here. I had hoped the same was not happening to your department, but clearly it has. Do you see the point in this, Special Agent, asking us to help save the world and then taking away our ability to do so?"

The general heard the response, the way that the voice stayed measured and even. He hadn't expected a break in the calm; that would never come. He had expected a more tailored response, and the general was prompted to ask another question.

"Is there someone there with you, Special Agent?"

It was even shorter this time, the confirmation of what he had suspected. The general, once again, did not care.

"Then I will be brief," the general said. "I know that this is suicide, Leo, and I know that you know it too. Every person under your command and mine will be dead in the next few days, as we send them into the horror that the rest of the world is trying to get away from. With so few of us, we do not stand a chance unless we have a real stroke of luck or genius. I will not abandon my troops or my mission, but I have no illusions about attaining a victory here. Leo, you are a good man. It has been a great honor to know you."

A few moments later, the general hung up the phone. He pressed a button on the device. His secretary's voice came through the intercom.

"Yes, sir?"

"There are ten special troops on their way here," the General told him. "When they arrive, I need you to see that they are processed as quickly as possible. Get them the same security clearance as I have, and bring them to me. Let all base personnel know that these people are to be treated as if they were me, and given the same respect and privileges. Set up a mandatory initial training session to begin immediately."

"Sir," the secretary cut him off, finally; the general had expected it. "I cannot authorize that kind of clearance, especially to that many people. If I could have their identification codes, I could get started with requesting the clearances."

"They aren't army," the general shook his head, although his secretary couldn't see him. "I doubt they will have any kind of identification or credentials when they arrive."

"How will we know them, sir?"

"They'll be wearing armor like you've never seen," the general allowed himself a small smile. "They'll have a million dollars worth of advanced weaponry attached to their special suits, and they are not to be challenged. One of them could bring this entire facility to its knees, if they cared to. Those are not the kind of credentials we need to see right now."

The secretary was silent, reluctant to speak his thoughts. The general went on, before he could.

"I'm sending you an emergency security clearance code right now," he pressed. "Use it to get them all badges, and gather all personnel."

"Sir?" The secretary was hesitant to question him yet again. "We have minimum personnel presence requirements for many sectors. Shall I set up training shift schedules?"

"I sent you the code," the general said. "Use it to put the cells on lockdown, all of them. Gather all personnel. Like the message says."

"Of course, sir," he responded. "It does not say how long to grant our guests full facility access."

"Permanently," the general sighed. "Or until further notice."

"Sir?" His voice quavered a little; if the general hadn't known him so well, he never would have noticed. "Are these people a threat?"

"No," the general replied resolutely. "They're our only hope."

* * *

"You're home early."

Tina moved to lift herself out of bed; the general stopped her.

"No, sweetheart," he said. "I need to get back soon."

The general lowered his weight to the mattress, and she scooted closer. Tina moved her hand into his; it looked old and withered, and her grip was weak when she squeezed his fingers. Her other hand pointed the remote control at the television; she was watching the world news. She already knew. With a click, the screen went blank and fell silent.

"Is this it, then?" Her body was failing her, but Tina's mind was as sharp as ever. She had never asked what they were waiting for, in all the years since he had been so suddenly elevated in rank; but she knew they were waiting for something, and that he had fervently hoped it would never come. He didn't have to answer; she had only gotten better at reading his mind in their time together. Tina sighed, squeezed his hand weakly once more, and spoke again.

"Are the families on base safe?" she asked.

There was no distress or insistency to her question; she might have been asking if he had enjoyed his lunch today.

The general shook his head, frowned.

"Can you leave me a gun?" she whispered.

"Tina, sweetheart." The general looked her in the eye for the first time since sitting down; he let her see the tears, and the hope lost. He went on.

"I think you should come back to HQ with me," he said. "I can keep you safe there. Leaving you with a handgun won't help you fight this threat."

Her other hand moved, slowly, to clasp his larger one. They both squeezed, weakly, and she smiled.

"I'm not fighting anything," she murmured. "I've been dwindling to nothing for a long time. I can barely make you dinner every night; it exhausts me for the entirety of the next day. I'm not a fighter, General; I never have been. I'm just a tired old lady who would rather meet her maker on her own terms."

He leaned over, and kissed her.

"I need to get back," he said. "I'm going to

grab a bite out of the fridge, and get washed up. I'll come kiss you goodbye before I go. Do you need anything?"

Tina shook her head, smiled softly.

"Just that kiss," she said. "I'll be here waiting."

The general went to the kitchen, found some cold tastelessness and forced himself to chew and swallow. He was tempted to wash it down with a beer, but that was a line even the zombie apocalypse would not make him cross. After he used the restroom, and washed up, the general went into the bedroom once more.

She was sleeping. He had watched her sleep many times over the years. When she was young, her beauty became an angelic peaceful countenance in slumber; as she got older, unconsciousness rolled back the clock and smoothed the worry lines. Now, she just looked tired. Even in sleep, her body was too exhausted to hold her mouth open or her neck straight. Tina's head lolled to one side, propped on the pillow, awaiting his kiss.

He knelt by the bedside, watching her as he let his hand go through the familiar motion. Tina didn't stir, or move; he opened the bedside drawer, quietly. Sliding the nine millimeter from its snug ankle holster, he chambered a round as silently as possible. When he closed the drawer she was awake, and watching him.

The general stood, and leaned over her. He covered her smile with his own, tasted the flavor of his love, and lingered there for a long moment. When he drew back, her smile had widened.

"Well, General!" Tina waved her withered hand in front of her tired face. "Keep that up, and you won't make it back to work at all!"

They laughed together, and he stood up straight. After their laughter died down, their eyes drifted to the nightstand at the same time.

"Thank you," she whispered. "I love you, General. So much."

"I love you, Tina," he blinked back his tears, saved them for the short trip to headquarters. "Get some good rest, sweetheart."

* * *

He watched his people train with the zombie killers for the next three days. The special agents brought the best out in them, and unified them more than ever under his command. Stories were whispered, at first;

then they were told in conversational tones, with cautious eyes on him. When the general neither confirmed nor denied them, the tales grew even taller. A couple people came eerily close to guessing what had happened, all those years ago; both events seemed to haunt him, as surely as the thought of a loaded pistol at Tina's bedside did.

Each evening she had dinner waiting for him; she even made him meatloaf one last time, and packed some in his cooler the next morning. She fussed over him like she hadn't in years those few days, helping him dress in the morning and telling him how handsome he looked. It clearly took its toll on her, but Tina brushed aside all of his concerns; it was as though she was trying to use up all the energy she had for her lifetime before it ended. They never spoke about the pistol again.

When the base was breached, he let people go get their families. Some were lost, but many made it back; the general went home, and wrapped Tina's body in the comforter. He mourned her, there at her bedside, for as long as he thought it was safe; then he told her goodbye, and returned to his other home. There had to be something he could do besides sit and wait; the facility was secure, particularly in lockdown; but he had seen these monsters hunt before. No lock made by a human could resist the mind and the strength of a zombie forever; if there were more of them than humans, it was only a matter of time before the safest sanctuaries were flushed out.

He sat in his office, racking his brain and going over every painful distant memory he had. The recent one was too much to consider. He had access to any kind of ground or air fleet he needed; the only thing he needed to know was where to take them. The general spent hours thinking, days wondering, until he finally made a difficult decision. Packing all the extra clips he had, he went to talk to research.

* * *

"Sir?" The doctor looked at him, her brow furrowing in confusion. "Are you saying what I think you're saying? You want me to turn one of them so you can...so you can talk to it, sir?"

"That's right," Roberts nodded. "Do we have any prisoners left?"

She shrugged. "I believe so. There won't be any need to turn someone for this, though; unless you have a specific prisoner in mind."

The doctor raised an eyebrow, in clinical curiosity.

Roberts shook his head.

"We have a patient in restraints already," she said. "He's in full howler mode, like you want. Would you like to see him?"

The general nodded.

She didn't move; instead she watched him, with that detached wondering look. At last, she spoke.

"If I may, sir," she ventured, "are you going to torture him?"

He met her eyes, held the doctor's gaze until she looked away.

"I've never tortured anyone," he said quietly.

"Are you prepared to, sir?" Her eyes were back on his. "If that is what it takes, I mean. I'm behind you, sir; but I hope that is not why you chose me to accompany you. I'm much more of a chemist than a biologist. The components fascinate me; the big picture turns my stomach a little too easily."

"Honestly," Roberts answered, "I hadn't really thought of it. Let's hope it doesn't come to that."

"Of course, sir." She sounded relieved.

The general wished he shared the feeling. Anxiety had plagued him in his younger years; long decades had worn the sharp edges off nearly any startling thought or event. Losing his wife and torturing someone all in one week seemed too much for even his hardened soul to bear. He nearly turned back, more than once, as they walked together.

The monster was secured to a table and straining at its straps. It watched them enter the room, rusted red eyes burning with hunger and hate. It pulled harder against the straps; they protested, but held.

The general approached the creature, as the doctor closed the door behind them. He looked down at it, frowning slightly.

"You used to be human," he muttered. "What happened?"

He didn't expect a response. The general knew what had happened, as best as he could understand. He just didn't know why.

The creature made a sound, something between a growl and a moan. The general realized that they were words.

"Nature," the howler grinned. "Nature happened."

The general moved closer.

"Why?" he asked. "Why did this happen?"

"Sir." The doctor touched his arm, tried to pull him back. "Be careful."

Roberts jerked away.

"I'm fine, Doctor," he snapped.

He turned to the howler again. It was still grinning.

"Why?" he demanded. "Why, dammit?"

The monster chuckled. It was a dark and wet sound, gravel and guts rubbing against one another.

"Why?" It showed him the teeth in its mouth, the rows of jagged biters hungry for his flesh. "Why does the coyote hunt the deer, or the lion prey on the coyote? The herd must be culled. We are here to feed on you, until there aren't enough to feed on. Come closer."

The general could smell the rotten flesh on its breath, could see the sinewy strands between its teeth. He drew back, glanced at the doctor.

"I'm sorry," he said. "I think I wasted your time."

She shrugged. "Lockdown has killed my social life, along with these things. I have the time to waste. Anything else you want to ask?"

Roberts shook his head.

"I don't think so," he said. "You?"

"No, sir," she frowned, stole a glance at the creature. She shuddered. "That thing gives me the creeps."

"Me, too." The general's hand fell on the doorknob.

"General?"

He stopped, looked over his shoulder. The monster's voice sounded different, more refined somehow. It was no longer taxing its restraints; the howler had lain back, and looked almost peaceful.

"General Roberts?" he asked.

The general turned, approached the table once more.

"That's right," he said. "How did you come to know my name?"

"I've been looking for you, sir." The creature's eyes still gleamed red, but the gleam seemed different.

"Is that right?" Roberts glanced at the doctor; she shrugged.

"Yes, sir." The monster leaned forward; the restraints held the lunge, although Roberts saw only earnestness in it.

"I need your help, sir," it said. "My name is..."

The monster trailed off, looked at the floor for a long moment.

"My name was John Mallory, before this

happened to me," it said.

"That's not true." The doctor inched forward, as close as she could get. "I've seen your papers. Your-"

"Not this body," the howler interjected. "This body is only housing my consciousness for a little while. We all share a hive mind, everyone that has eaten flesh and turned to this. I discovered a way to overcome other minds, and inhabit their bodies for awhile. I can also fry them if need be, short circuit them in a manner of speaking."

"Are you saying-" The doctor was speaking slowly; he cut her off again.

"I'm saying that I am what happened to Doctor Cho," he nodded. "I apologize for that. And for interrupting. I would be more polite if I had more time. Which is exactly what I want to ask for. General, I will come to you, in my own body, at nightfall. I will wave a white flag, and you can choose to cut me down or let me in."

The general exchanged a glance with the doctor.

"And what happens," she asked, "if the general lets you in?"

"We'll work together," the howler said. "We'll chop off the head of this snake, and see if the body dies with it."

"What do you mean?" she pressed him.

The creature twitched, then spasmed; his eyes rolled back into his head. When they shifted to gaze at them again, they were once again blazing with hunger.

"Come closer," the monster hissed.

It was the same voice they had heard before; whatever had been there talking to them was gone. Roberts raised an eyebrow, patted his pistol.

"Do you mind?" he asked. "I have a feeling that we don't want this thing poking around in its own mind, or broadcasting anything that might not have already been shared."

She looked at the monster, then at him. The doctor nodded.

"I wish you would," she breathed.

The General lifted his hands to his ears, briefly. She nodded, and followed suit. The doctor's hands stayed over her ears while his fell; one snatched the pistol from his hip and put two bullets in the creature's skull. Both of its eyes were hollow caverns dripping blood as they turned together.

"Any new progress in the lab?" he asked, pacing her down the hallway. She nodded, smiled slightly.

"You know about the anonymous

message we received, right?" she asked. The general nodded. "We think it came from the lab department at the zombie killers secret headquarters. We tried to get back to them; no one responded to our messages. More importantly, we experimented with the data they sent. It seems to be legitimate, sir."

The general slowed his pace, looked at her.

"Do you have time to explain it to me?" he asked.

She nodded. "I'm off duty, sir. Besides, the cultures are undergoing a number of processes that take considerable time. I can't verify the claims put forth in the message for another twenty-four hours."

They stopped in front of his office.

"You're off duty," he said. "You should get some rest."

She looked at him quizzically.

"Is there any way I can wait with you until nightfall?" she ventured. "It's not far away, and I'm not apt to drift off knowing a zombie is going to knock on our front door any minute. If you don't mind me asking, sir, what are you going to do?"

He heaved a heavy sigh; there was no one to call for advice on this.

"I've got a six pack of Devil's Brew Stout

Ale in my office." He checked his watch. "I'll only have one, even if I am technically off duty. You are free to have at the other five if you will help me figure that out."

She looked alarmed.

"Or explain the chemistry of this thing in words I might understand," he proffered.

She beamed. "That I can do. I was terrified that those beers would be forever out of reach for me. Not that I'm a lush, or anything; I just-"

He laughed, for the first time in days.

"It's okay, Doctor," he said, keying open the door to his office. "All things considered, I can't believe so many of us are still sober."

*        *        *


A knock sounded on the door; their time together had passed too quickly. The general had seen her smile, and relax; he had felt himself forget what was happening outside the electrified fence for a while, and had even laughed a few more times. Neither of them brought up the fact that they would not be talking like this if the world wasn't ending outside.

They shared one last glance; he set his bottle on the desk, called out.

"Come in."

The door opened; his secretary stood erect, dark circles under his eyes. His family was in a state far away, and likely gone; he told the general that the work helped, so Roberts gave him plenty. It didn't matter that none of it would ever be filed, or read.

"Sir, you told me to expect a visitor." The young man barely moved.

Roberts glanced at his watch, sighed. He stood behind his desk, checking the sidearm at his hip.

"Thank you," he said. "I'm coming."

"Sir." The doctor stood abruptly. "What are you going to do?"

"I'm going to go talk to him."

"General, sir," the secretary frowned. "It's a howler, sir. The biggest I've ever seen. It's not the only one, either, sir; the building is surrounded. If you step outside that gate, they'll overwhelm you. You can't go out there alone."

"I'm not." The general patted his holstered companion. "Besides, I won't go past the gate. We're not shutting off that electricity for anyone, and I'm not letting a howler in without some serious restraints. Don't worry; just watch with the others on camera. If it does anything shifty, or you see me give a decisive signal, take it out. Otherwise treat this as an arranged meeting between diplomats, and stay back."

"Sir," he said, out of habit more than certainty. "Yes, sir."

The doctor hesitated at the doorway.

"Come if you want," Roberts nodded.

"Sir," she smiled, slightly. "Thank you, sir."

They rode the elevator and traversed the hallways in silence; they were both afraid to ask the other to express their thoughts, or to voice their own. He spoke to her as the door opened, and they tasted the chill night air for the first time in days.

"They need to lock up behind us," he cautioned her. "You can turn back now, if you don't want to be locked outside with me and..."

"John Mallory, sir," she said. "He said that his name is John Mallory. Let's go see what he has to say."

They moved through the doorway, walked quietly together once more. He could see the white flag through the fence, and the red eyes that glowed in the distance. There were too many to count, lighting up the night like a macabre holiday yard display. One pair glowed over the white flag, larger and brighter than the rest.

"General?"

The voice was almost human; not quite, but almost. The general nodded as he approached the live wire, called back.

"Mister Mallory," he said. "Thank you for coming."

"Thank you, sir, for meeting with me." The creature was even more monstrous up close. Roberts was surprised at how near the doctor came to the fence. The howler acknowledged her with a nod.

"Doctor Goldstein," he growled. "I apologize for what I did to your associate, and for being rude to you earlier."

She nodded. "I understand, Professor."

They both reacted to the title; Roberts looked at her, curious, while the howler laughed. She held up her portable wireless device.

"The internet is back up," she said. "I searched him. He was a professor at-"

"Now I must interrupt again." The creature was still laughing, a low rumbling chuckle that sounded as much like a growl as a laugh. "I am not here on my past credentials. I am here as what I am, one of the first wave of this catastrophe that is pounding the Earth. I may know how to stop this. With your help."

"Why would you?" The general raised an eyebrow. "Don't you all think and act as one?"

The howler shook his head.

"I severed that connection, General," the creature said. Pride shone in his eyes, along with intelligence. "I don't let the hive mind into mine anymore. I can still feel it, at the corners of my consciousness, and I can still leap into it at will like I did earlier; but as far as I can tell, my thoughts are my own again. It happened when I went against the hive mind recently. I was able to shut out those desires to fulfill a deeper desire of my own."

"Oh?" The general was curious. "And what desire was that?"

"To save my daughter." The howler dropped his gaze to the ground.

"And now you want to save the world?" The general smiled at him, a sad smile that had kindness in it.

"If a hurricane is coming at me," the monster murmured. "I can scream at it, or run, or throw stones, or lay down and wait for death. They may all end up the same, in the end; I know that. I'm still here to throw my stones, sir."

"We've got more than stones here," the

general said. "But if we start throwing them with no objective, we will exhaust our stores and face the same plight as the rest of the world."

A wicked gleam lit the monster's eyes.

"Can you get your weapons to Egypt?" he asked. "The head of the snake is there. If we cut it off..."

The general let his eyes wander the shadows behind the monster.

"We may use everything we've got just trying to get to the airfield," he pointed out. "You aren't the only howler waiting for us to open these gates. How do we get past that?"

The monster looked over its shoulder. One creature ran forward, from the shadows into the light. It headed for the electrified fence at a full clip. Suddenly, thirty feet from the fence, it tumbled to the ground as if struck by a fatal blow. Its body lie still after it stopped tumbling, and another creature ran forth. It lost all function as the first had, collapsing into a lifeless heap and rolling to a dead stop. The howler turned, met the general's eyes.

"You did that?" The general's voice was touched with awe.

The creature nodded. "And this."

Dozens of howls filled the air behind the

giant monster. Footsteps pounded the earth, and a score of them came charging at the fence; as one, they fell. The lights went out in their eyes, and they dropped lifeless to the ground. Roberts eyed the bodies, then the night beyond the fence. There was only one set of glowing red eyes remaining; they were full of intelligence and hope and yearning.

The doctor gasped.

"How did you do that?" she breathed.

The monster shrugged sinewy shoulders.

"A lot of prep work," he admitted. "If I could do it that easily, I would scour the globe taking down howlers. These were hungry, and very far away from the proverbial head of the snake. The best I'll be able to do as we get closer is keep them from attacking. The smarter ones drift to better hunting grounds when fresh flesh gets sparse. Sorry, doctor."

The general glanced at her; her face had twisted at the hunting and feeding references, and was only now relaxing.

"It's okay," she tried to smile. "We all eat something."

"This snake you keep mentioning," Roberts said, "tell me more about it. What makes you think we can cut off the head?"

"I was speaking metaphorically, General," the howler responded. "The hive mind is a huge network stretching across the globe. It all leads back to one place, to one person. She is responsible for me being the way I am, for all of those turned in the first wave."

"How many were turned in the first wave?" the doctor demanded.

"Four," the howler answered. "There were four of us. We were consumed with hunger, and the flesh falling from our bodies was infectious as well. We went all over the world, and spread this awful thing. We four are the ones responsible for what has happened here, as much as her; but if we stop her, this all might be over."

"Like killing the head vampire?" The doctor was nearly shouting. "What do you think this is, a horror movie? We're in the middle of an apocalypse here! Is there any reason to think this will work?"

Silence reigned for several seconds, while her anxious cries drifted away into the night.

"Like I said," the monster offered, quietly. "I'm just throwing stones."

"Would you suffer wearing some restraints?" Roberts raised an eyebrow. "I don't think I can bring you in any other way."

"General," the doctor frowned. "In here? You want to bring him in here?"

The howler nodded.

"You'll get that response from most of your people," he said. "I take no offense. I know I am a monster. I will wait nearby; if you wish to help me, I will be around until tomorrow night. After that, I must try to do this on my own. Too many people are dying."

Roberts snatched the radio from his belt, tossed it nearly straight up into the air. It peaked high over the electrified barbed wire coiled at the top of the fence, and fell to the other side. The howler moved to catch it, a blur of talons and fangs that was a terrifying wonder to watch.

"Keep that on," Roberts called out. "Radio me on that channel before you go anywhere. I'll have another one on in a few minutes. Don't disappear on me, Mallory."

The creature nodded, and drifted into the shadows. It was as natural and chilling as watching him move to catch the radio; one moment he was there, and the next he was gone.

The doctor turned to him.

"Sir?" she asked. "Are we going to go with him?"

He squeezed the bridge of his nose between thumb and forefinger, frowning.

"I don't know, Doctor," he admitted.

"I have been desperately searching for something we can do, anything. Hell, I'm not ashamed to say that I've prayed about it."

"Did you think the answer to your prayers would be a flesh-eating zombie, sir?" she quipped.

He let his hand fall to his side, returned her slight smile.

"No, Doctor," he admitted. "I never imagined that."

Dear Reader,

And that's the set! I hope you loved the stories, and my interludes. It's probably worth mentioning that there is another tie-in to these stories. The fourth volume in this set will be called 'The Zombie Killers', and it will feature the crew that came in to train the general's troops.

They have some pretty interesting stories to tell, those twelve. You'll find three of them in 'The Zombie Killers'. They also show up in 'Zombie Zero: The First Zombie'. In fact... oh, I shouldn't say any more.

If you want to find out more of what I joyfully endured writing these stories, you might consider signing up for my newsletter. It's free to join, and you get a weekly message, free content and access to giveaways. This year the focus is on these short stories, and rewarding subscribers for their support.

One of the most helpful things you can do for many authors is review their books. If you enjoyed this book, or even if you didn't, I would sincerely appreciate if you took a few minutes to leave an honest review.

There are a few great sites to post on, the most noteworthy being Amazon.com and Goodreads.com.

Reviews are a great way to help authors and readers find each other, and they benefit both sides of the page tremendously. If you want some help with writing a book review, I wrote a tutorial on my website to help you get started.

Most of all, I appreciate that fact that you are reading this in the first place. I don't say that I hope you enjoy these stories so much because I forget that I've said it already; I say it because I mean it every time. Writing my books is only the first step in my dreams all coming true; it ends with readers like you looking forward to reading more, and trusting my name on the cover to mean great stories inside.

Finally, I want to make sure that you know that you have direct access to me. If you want to let me know how much you loved a tie-in, or yell at me for letting someone awesome die, you can always message me. I'm a busy guy, so be patient... but I'll get back to you. That's why I left you my e-mail address, under my name down there. Thanks for reading!

All the best,

Jay

Jay@JayNorry.com

Twitter: @JayNorry